THE TALKING
MICKEY MOUSE SHOW™

The
Magic
Boomerang

W•W
WORLDS OF WONDER™

© MCMLXXXVI The Walt Disney Company. ℗ MCMLXXXVI Buena Vista Distribution Co., Inc. All rights reserved. Worlds of Wonder, Inc. is the exclusive licensee, manufacturer and distributor of The Talking Mickey Mouse Show toys. Mickey Mouse and Mickey Mouse characters are trademarks of The Walt Disney Company, Burbank, California. The symbol W•W and "Worlds of Wonder" are trademarks of Worlds of Wonder, Inc., Fremont, California.

Printed in U.S.A. / P35

ISBN: 1-55578-302-3

Mickey   I love to get the mail every day, don't you? One day Donald Duck, our mailman, delivered a special surprise.

Donald   I have a letter all the way from Australia, Mickey.

Goofy   Australia! Gawrsh, Mickey, it must be from your Uncle Digger.

Donald   I've got it right here in my bag. Here you go.

Mickey   Pluto, what are you doing! Down, boy!

Goofy   Gawrsh, Donald, Pluto snatched that letter right out of your hand!

Donald   For cryin' out loud! What's the matter with him?

Mickey   I'm sorry, Donald. I forgot we've been teaching Pluto to fetch. Give me the letter, boy.

Goofy   What does it say, Mick?

Mickey   Gee, this is strange. Uncle Digger says he needs his boomerang back—you know, the one he sent me a long time ago. Goofy, I gave that to you. Do you know where it is?

Goofy   I think it's up in my attic somewhere, Mick. I never did get the knack of throwing it. Let's go look.

Mickey Pretty soon we were rummaging around Goofy's attic.

Goofy Here 'tis! I never throw anything away. Where does your uncle want us to send it?

Mickey The letter just says *General delivery, Boolaboola*. Say, here's a funny thing I didn't notice before—a row of dots and dashes under his signature. It could be code, and if it is, it spells S-O-S!

Goofy Isn't that what ships say when they're in trouble?

Mickey It sure is. Uncle Digger could be giving us a message. There's only one way to find out—deliver this boomerang ourselves! Australia, here we come!

Goofy   A few days later, Mickey and I landed at Boolaboola. That's in what they call the Australian bush country.

Mickey   Let's head for town and get settled at the hotel, Goof. Then we can check with the post office about delivering the boomerang to Uncle Digger.

Goofy   You know, Mick, this place sort of reminds me of our old West—except for the kangaroos.

Goofy   The clerk at the post office told us Mickey's Uncle Digger had come out of retirement kinda unexpectedly and headed back into the bush.

Clerk   I haven't seen Digger since that day, but one of his partners comes in every week and picks up his supplies and mail. In fact, that's his partner over there, right across the street.

Mickey   C'mon, Goof. Let's go talk to him. If there's nothing wrong, he won't mind telling us where Uncle Digger is.

Mickey Beg your pardon, sir. My name's Mickey Mouse, and this is Goofy. We're looking for my Uncle Digger, and I understand you're his partner.

Cobber That's right, mate. Cobber's the name.

Goofy Could you tell us where Uncle Digger is?

Cobber He's over at Kookaburra Springs. I'd guide you out, but I've got business in the other direction. You can't miss it, though. Just follow the trail out of town for about ten miles.

Mickey   Goofy and I hired some horses and headed out, taking the boomerang with us. Pretty soon the trail narrowed down to just a slit in the rocks.

Goofy   You know, Mick, this reminds me of a Western movie I saw once. The hero was riding through a gap just like this, and the bad guy was on top of the cliff ready to roll a big boulder down on him. The hero just happened to look up and saw a shadow on the other cliff. Just like that one up there!

Mickey   Holy cow! Let's get out of here, Goof!

Goofy   Gawrsh! Faster, Mickey! That boulder's headin' straight
for us! Whoa!

Mickey   Don't stop, Goofy!

Goofy   Wh-who's stopping? Yeow!

Mickey   The boulder crashed down just a few inches behind Goofy's horse! Up above, the mysterious man on the cliff watched us ride off.

Cobber   Bah! They got away! What blasted luck! Well, I'd better get down to camp. I'll show them there's a trick or two left up ol' Cobber's sleeve.

Mickey   That was a close call, Goofy. There's no doubt about it, Uncle Digger's S-O-S was for real. Someone doesn't want us to reach Kookaburra Springs.

Goofy   You know, we were in such a hurry to get away, I think we've lost the trail.

Mickey   We'd better try and get our bearings.

Goofy   Look, Mick, smoke. Maybe there'll be some folks there who could help us.

Mickey	Let's sneak up quietly, Goof. We don't want to walk into any more traps.
Goofy	We're in luck! The sign says *Tourist Information*. Come on, Mick, let's see if anybody's around.
Mickey	Wait, Goofy! It sounds sort of fishy. Oh well, I guess it's all right.
Goofy	You know, Mick, walkin' into town like this kinda reminds me of another Western movie, where the hero was huntin' the bad guys' hideout. Now let's see, how did that go?

Cobber I'll tell you how it went—the bad guy puts up a fake sign. I saw that picture, too.

Mickey It's Cobber!

Cobber I'd say that trap works pretty well. Hands up, mates, and welcome to Kookaburra Springs.

Cobber Now gents, I'll take the boomerang and introduce you to my real partner. Alf, come out here and tie these guys up. And bring ol' Digger out of the cabin with you.

Mickey Uncle Digger, are we glad to see you! What's this all about?

Goofy Yeah, why did you want the boomerang back?

Digger I didn't want it back. *They* did. These villains nabbed my pet kangaroo, Hoppity, and threatened to harm her unless I wrote to you to return the boomerang.

Cobber That's right, Digger. Now if you want to see Hoppity and your friends here set free, you'd better get busy finding gold with this thing.

Mickey Uncle Digger, your boomerang can find gold?

Digger Yes. It's made out of a rare, ancient wood that's attracted by gold. Years ago I saved a native's life. He gave me the boomerang.

Goofy Gawrsh, can anybody find gold with it?

Digger No, the native also taught me the special throw it needs. Very few people have the knack to throw it right. I haven't tried it in quite some time, but here it goes.

Mickey Uncle Digger threw the boomerang, and it sailed off.
Goofy Wow, look at it go. I never could get it to fly like that. Hey, it's changing direction and landing on that hill.
Cobber That means there's gold there! Come on!
Goofy Huh, I thought a boomerang was supposed to come back to the fella that throws it.

Mickey Cobber and Alf made us all run up the hill where Uncle Digger's boomerang had spun down.

Goofy Look, Mick, it landed right next to a great big gold nugget!

Cobber We're rich, Alf, we're rich!

Goofy Gawrsh, Mr. Digger, that's quite a throwing arm you have there.

Mickey   So the boomerang *does* work!

Digger   That's right, nephew. I used to love prospecting this way, but now I'm sick and tired of it.

Goofy   Gee, Uncle Digger, don't you need any more gold?

Digger   The boomerang helped me find all the gold I needed to retire in peace, but people never stop pestering me to find more gold for them.

Cobber   That's right, and I'm ready to find some more! Get busy!

Mickey   Uncle Digger wound up for another throw, then he winced and the boomerang clunked down a few feet away.

Goofy   Are you okay, Uncle Digger?

Cobber   What happened? Where's our gold?

Digger   It's your fault, Cobber. It's been so long since I used this thing that I overdid it and threw my arm out. It'll be at least a couple of days before I can throw again.

Mickey You should have seen how red Cobber's face got then.
Cobber Rats! All that gold waiting to be picked up, and we have to sit around until your arm heals.
Digger Listen, maybe we can work something out. If you let my friends go, I'll teach you how to throw the boomerang.
Cobber That's a great idea. You've got a deal, mate.
Goofy Gawrsh, Uncle Digger, are you sure you want to do that?

Mickey   Uncle Digger gave us a wink as he led Cobber to a good throwing spot.

Digger   Now, throw it over those trees as hard as you can.

Cobber   Like this?

Goofy   Wow, Mick, look at 'er go!

Digger   Good throw, Cobber! Now don't move so we can hear where it lands.

Cobber   I don't hear anything.

Digger   Don't worry, you'll hear birdies in a second.

Mickey   All of a sudden, the boomerang came flying in and whacked Cobber on the back of the head! He was knocked out cold.

Goofy   That's when Mickey went into action. He jumped Alf and knocked him to the ground. Then Uncle Digger grabbed Cobber.

Mickey   Uncle Digger, isn't your arm hurt?

Digger   No, I was just faking so Cobber would throw that thing. I had a hunch he'd forget that a boomerang usually returns to the thrower.

Goofy   We rescued Hoppity, then headed for town and turned Cobber and Alf over to the Boolaboola police.

Mickey   Well, Uncle Digger, your troubles are over. Hoppity is safe, and those two won't be bothering anyone for a long time.

Digger   I wish it were that easy, nephew. People will always be after me to find gold as long as I have this boomerang.

Goofy   Can't you burn it up or somethin'?

Digger   My goodness, no! The old native who gave it to me said there'd be a curse on anyone who destroyed it! I thought sending it far away to you fellows was the answer, but even that didn't work.

Mickey   Then what are you going to do, Uncle Digger?

Digger   There's only one thing I can do—leave Australia and go someplace where nobody knows me.

Goofy   Gawrsh, that's a shame.

Digger   Listen, lads, before we leave, I'd like to use this boomerang one more time to repay you for all your trouble.

Mickey   You don't have to do that, Uncle Digger.

Digger   I insist. Follow me and Hoppity. We'll go outside of town a ways and look for a likely spot.

Mickey   Soon we were watching the boomerang fly through the air again.
Goofy   It's landing in the middle of that brush, Mick.
Mickey   Come on, let's go find it.

Mickey   Goofy ran on ahead of us.

Goofy   Over here, fellas! Here 'tis. It landed right on an old anthill.

Digger   And here's your gold, lads. Help yourselves.

Mickey   Wow, there's enough here to pay for our trip and then some.

Digger   Hey, would you look at this? My boomerang's disappearing right before my eyes!

Mickey Disappearing? How can that be?

Digger My troubles are over! This isn't an anthill. It's a termite mound!

Goofy Gawrsh! But what about the curse?

Digger It's on the termites, not me. Now I can retire in peace.

Mickey Well, I guess it's time for us to leave Australia—right, Goofy? Goofy, what are you doing?

Goofy Hey, Mick, I can hop just like Hoppity!

Mickey But you're not a kangaroo.

Goofy I'm just practicin' for our long *hop* home!